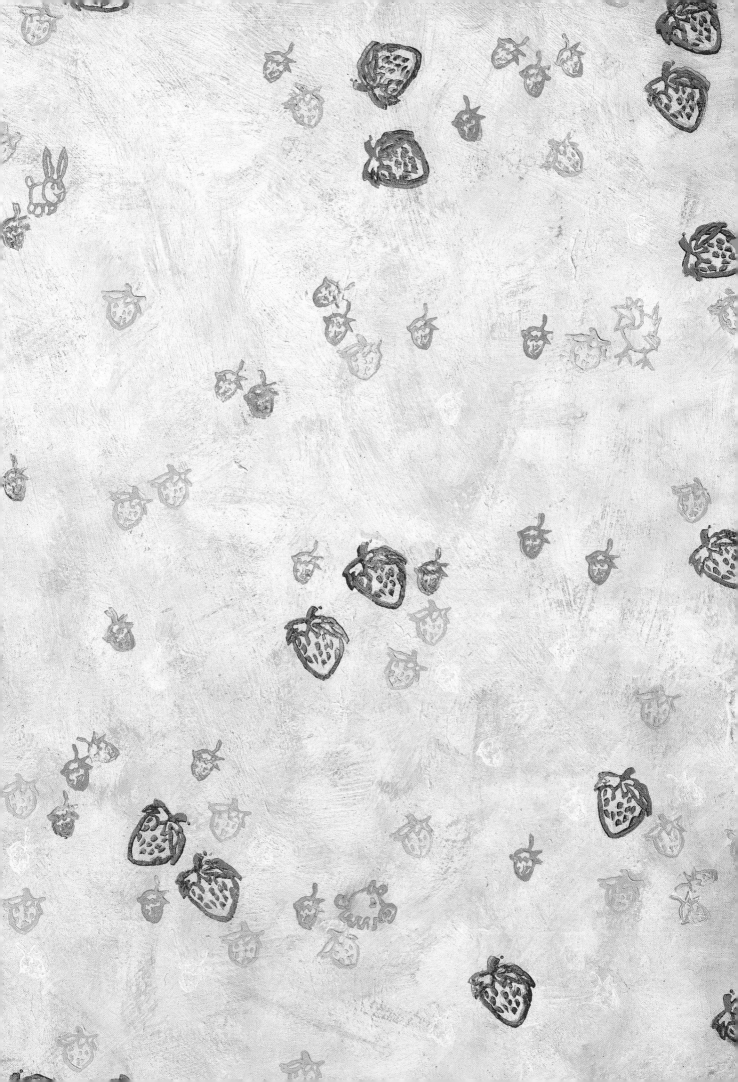

Copyright © 2002 by Michael Neugebauer Verlag, an imprint of
Nord-Süd Verlag AG, Gossau Zürich, Switzerland
First published in Switzerland under the title *Wo ist Bodo?*

First published in the United States, Great Britain, Canada,
Australia, and New Zealand in 2002 by North-South Books,
an imprint of Nord-Süd Verlag AG, Gossau Zürich, Switzerland.

Distributed in the United States by North-South Books Inc., New York.

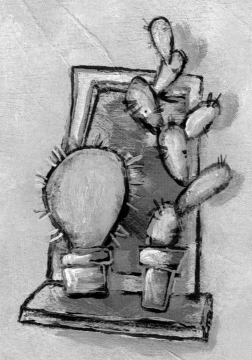

Library of Congress Cataloging-in-Publication Data is available.
A CIP catalogue record for this book is available from The British Library.
ISBN 0-7358-1618-2 (trade edition)   10 9 8 7 6 5 4 3 2 1
ISBN 0-7358-1619-0 (library edition)   10 9 8 7 6 5 4 3 2 1

Printed in Belgium

For more information about our books, and the authors and artists
who create them, visit our web site: www.northsouth.com

WHERE IS HENRY?

BY
CHARISE NEUGEBAUER

ILLUSTRATED BY
MICHAEL WREDE

A MICHAEL NEUGEBAUER BOOK
North-South Books
New York / London

Henry had come to visit Uncle Humphrey.
He loved spending time with his uncle and
his uncle loved spending time with him.

"Let's have some ice cream," said Uncle Humphrey.
"Oh, yes!" Henry replied. His mouth was watering.
"I'll go and pick some strawberries
 to eat with the ice cream."
"Good idea," Uncle Humphrey agreed.

Henry filled his bucket with luscious red strawberries.
He couldn't resist tasting a few. Suddenly, he heard a voice.

"Ready or not, here I come."

Someone was playing hide-and-seek!

Willy, Laura, and Tony were all at the big tree,
ready to start another round of the game.
"Hello there," said Henry. "I'm Henry,
Humphrey's nephew. Can I play too?"

"You!" cried Laura. "Of course not! You are much too fat."
The others laughed. Then they all chanted:

*"Big and fat and oh, so wide,
There's nowhere you could ever hide!"*

Sadly, Henry headed back to Uncle Humphrey's house.

"There you are!" said Uncle Humphrey.
"Come on, let's have our ice cream now."

But Henry couldn't eat. He started to cry.
"I shouldn't have this ice cream," he said, sobbing.
"I'm much too fat! That's why no one wants to play with me."
Humphrey patted Henry's back.
Then he asked him what had happened.

Outside, the game of hide-and-seek continued. Laura had hidden behind the wheelbarrow. That's where she always hid. And, of course, Willy had won again.

"This is boring," said Tony.
"We should find a new place to play."
"Oh, yes!" the others said, and they raced off.

When they came to Humphrey's garden, Willy said,
"This would be perfect."
"Yes," agreed Tony. "There are lots of good hiding places here."
"We have to ask first," said Laura.

Humphrey saw them standing by his fence.
He had a wonderful idea.

Laura knocked on the door.
"Come in!" called Humphrey.
They stepped inside, but they couldn't see anyone.
"Where are you, Humphrey?" they called.

"Here I am!" Humphrey replied.
"Here I am, too!" called Henry.
Laura, Tony, and Willy found Humphrey in the sitting room.

"Hello, Humphrey," said Laura.
"Could we use your garden to play—"
"Hide-and-seek!" said Henry.
"Is that Henry?" Laura asked, confused.
She looked all around the room. "Where is Henry?"
"I'm right in front of you!" said Henry.

Tony looked under the bed, Willy checked
behind the door, and Laura peeked behind the chair.
They looked for Henry in all the hiding places
they could think of.
Where on earth could he be hiding?

Henry couldn't help it.
He just had to laugh.
And that's how they found him.

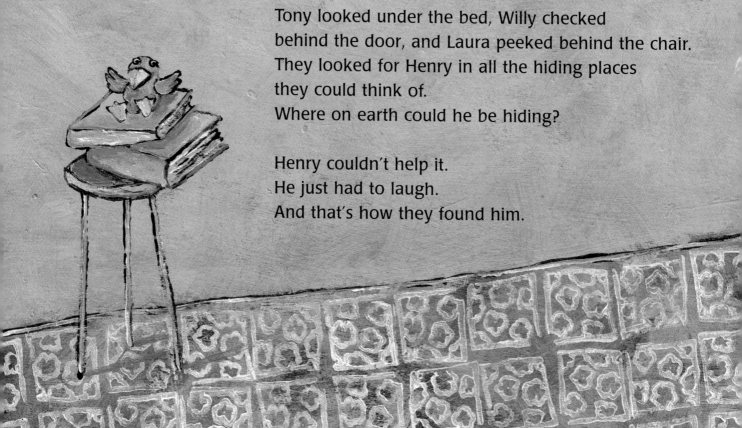

"You found me!" he called happily.
"Last one to the big tree is it!"
They all raced outside.

"I'm it," said Laura. "You three hide."
Then she and Willy and Tony all chanted:

"He is nice and he is fun.
He hides better than anyone!"

The game continued all afternoon.
And Henry played along with his new friends.

Finally Humphrey called to them.
"Time to go home now. Your parents will be worried."
"Okay," said Laura. "But first you have to find us."

Humphrey laughed. He covered his eyes,
counted to ten, and called,
"Ready or not,
here I come!"